To Sarah Mei and Sophie Hui – KU
For Annika – GA

A TEMPLAR BOOK

First published in the UK in 2016 by Templar Publishing,
part of the Bonnier Publishing Group,
The Plaza, 535 King's Road, London, SW10 0SZ
www.templarco.co.uk
www.bonnierpublishing.com

Text copyright © Kaye Umansky 2016
Illustration copyright © Greg Abbott 2016

1 3 5 7 9 10 8 6 4 2

ISBN 978-1-78370-381-4 (Hardback)
IBSN 978-1-78370-574-0 (Paperback)

Designed by Genevieve Webster
Edited by Alison Ritchie

Printed in China

NAUGHTY *Naughty* MONSTER

WRITTEN BY KAYE UMANSKY

Illustrated by Greg Abbott

templar publishing

The Naughty, Naughty Monster
Came rampaging through the wood,
Scaring all the little animals.
He wasn't being good.

"I'm a Naughty, Naughty Monster!
Are you ready? Here I come!
I am hungry for my dinner
And I want you in my tum!"

The tiny woodland creatures
Shook and shivered in their holes;
The rabbits and the dormice
And the hedgehogs and the moles.

The Monster sniffed and snuffled,
He was searching high and low,
When he heard a word,
A crisp, sharp word;
That crisp, sharp word was . . .

. . . "NO!"

Before him stood a Fairy,

With a head of yellow curls

And a fancy gold tiara

And a necklace made of pearls.

The sweetest little Fairy

You could ever hope to see,

Except for her expression,

Which was cross as cross can be.

"Naughty, Naughty Monster!
What a wicked thing to do!
Stop scaring little creatures
Who have done no harm to you!

I am sending you straight home again.
Be off! Back to your cave!
And don't you dare come out
Until you've learned how to behave."

But the Naughty, Naughty Monster
Came rampaging through the farm,
Causing squeaky-squawky flapping,
Consternation and alarm.

"I'm a Naughty, Naughty Monster!
Are you ready? Here I come!
I am hungry for my dinner
And I want you in my tum."

All the frightened farmyard animals
Were quaking in their pens.
The piglets were quite petrified
And so were all the hens.

There was terror in the stable,
There was panic in the dairy . . .

But everything calmed down
With the arrival of the Fairy.

"Naughty, Naughty Monster!
You do not know wrong from right!
It's back into your cave
Until you learn to be polite!"

But the Naughty, Naughty Monster
Came rampaging up the street!
He was kicking over dustbins
With his massive monster feet.

"I'm a Naughty, Naughty Monster!
Are you ready? Here I come!
I am hungry for my dinner
And I want you in my tum!"

Oh, the panic! The confusion!
So much shouting, so much noise,
From the mummies and the daddies
And the frightened girls and boys.

The Monster was enjoying it,
And loving acting tough.
Not the goody-goody Fairy, though –
She'd really had enough.

"Naughty, Naughty Monster!
You will not do as I say,
So it's back into your cave with you,
And in that cave YOU'LL STAY!

I am blocking up the entrance
With a great big, heavy stone,
And that will be your punishment,
To stay there, all alone."

He'd really gone and done it now.
He couldn't shift the boulder,
Though he kicked it and he thumped it
And he shoved it with his shoulder.

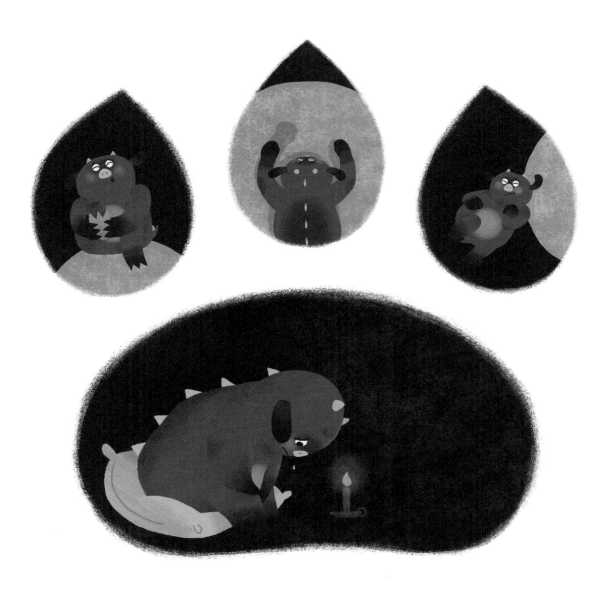

He slumped down on a cushion
And he shed a little tear.
He'd go no more a-monstering.
That much was plainly clear.

The days passed very slowly,

It was not a lot of fun.

He had lots of time to think about
The naughty things he'd done.

He got paper, pen and envelope
And wrote a little note,
In his best and neatest writing,
This is what he wrote . . .

Dear Fairy, (wrote the Monster)

I am writing you a letter.
I know that I was naughty,
But I think I'm getting better.

I am very, very sorry,
And I promise to be good.
Please come and let me out again.
I really wish you would.

XXX

The letter was delivered
By a helpful little bird,
And a very happy Fairy
Sat and read it. Every word.

She really hoped he meant it,
Though she had a bit of doubt,
But decided he deserved a chance
And kindly let him out.

The Naughty,
Naughty Monster
went rampaging
through the wood . . .

. . . Hugging all the little animals
And being rather GOOD.

He visited the farm,
Where he was friendly, kind and sweet.
He handed out red roses
To the people in the street!

"I'm a Funny, Friendly Monster!
Just as nice as nice can be.
Take a flower! Have a cuddle!
Come on home and have some tea."

It took some getting used to
And it felt a little strange,
Being Nice instead of Naughty –
But it made a pleasant change.

The Fairy was delighted
When she saw him making friends.
She took a rose and kissed his nose.
And there the story ends.

Though sometimes, in his dreams at night,
He still acts rough and scary
And is very, very naughty.

But we will not tell the Fairy.

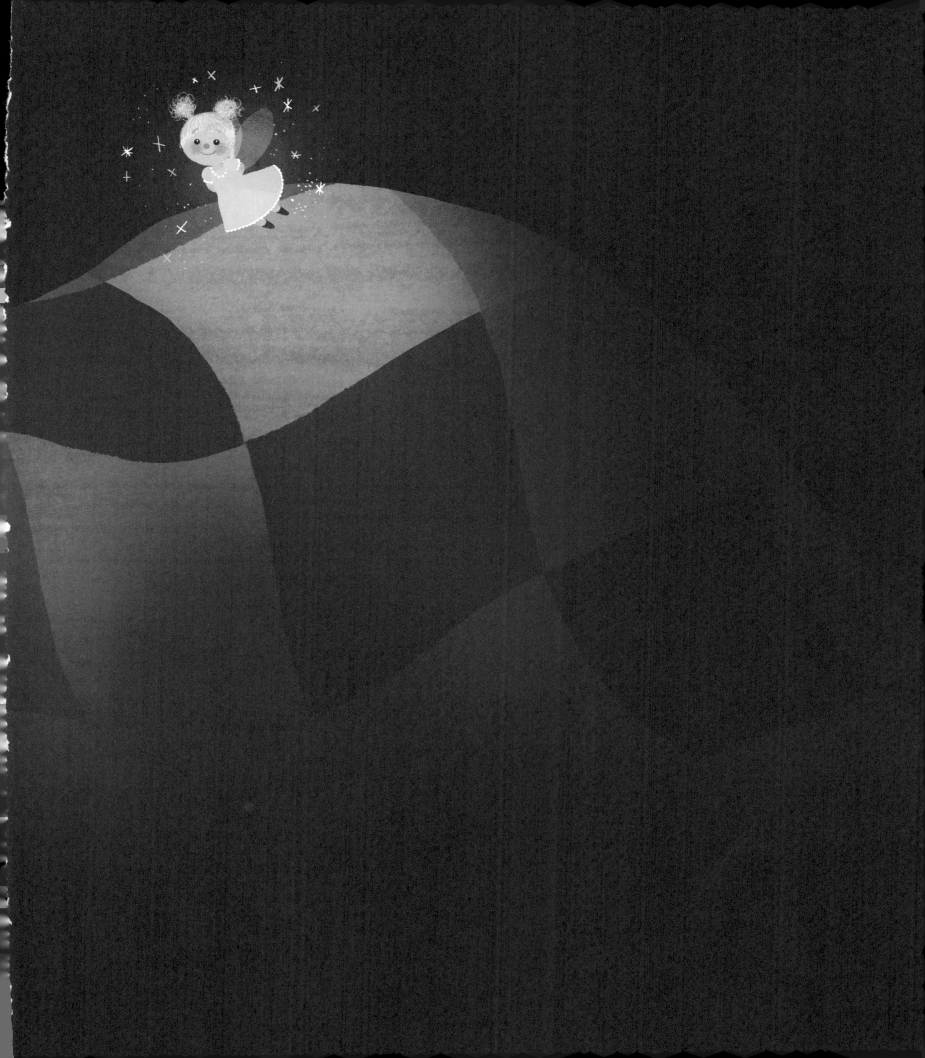